STANDING ON NEPTUNE

Selected stories for Tweens and Teens
by Valerie Sherrard

Birdspell
"*Birdspell* offers remarkable insight to young readers unfamiliar
with mental health issues ... compelling and compassionate ... a very
readable book laced with humour and grace."
— Charis Cotter, *Quill & Quire*

A Bend in the Breeze
Sheree Fitch's "favourite NB book" choice.
"The characters were quirky, fun, and interesting. The world
Sherrard creates is believable, curious and joyful, yet full
of human imperfection and emotion."
— Chris Benjamin, *Atlantic Books Today*

The Glory Wind
Rain Shadow
Driftwood
Tumbleweed Skies

If you like to laugh:
The Rise and Fall of Derek Cowell
Random Acts
Speechless

Non-Fiction
(with Natalie Hyde and David Jardine)
More than Words: Navigating the Complex World of Communication

STANDING ON NEPTUNE

ON

NEPTUNE

VALERIE SHERRARD

We acknowledge financial support for our publishing activities: the Government
of Canada, through the Canada Book Fund and The Canada Council for the Arts;
the Government of Ontario, through the Ontario Arts Council, Ontario Creates, and
the Ontario Book Publishing Tax Credit. We acknowledge additional funding
provided by the Government of Ontario and the Ontario Arts Council to
address the adverse effects of the novel coronavirus pandemic.

Library and Archives Canada Cataloguing in Publication

Title: Standing on Neptune / Valerie Sherrard.
Names: Sherrard, Valerie, author.
Identifiers: Canadiana (print) 20230146910 | Canadiana (ebook) 20230146929 |
ISBN 9781770866874 (softcover) | ISBN 9781770866881 (HTML)
Subjects: LCGFT: Novels in verse.
Classification: LCC PS8587.H3867 S73 2023 | DDC jC813/.6—dc23

United States Library of Congress Control Number: 2023930403

Cover art: David Jardine
Interior text design: Marijke Friesen
Manufactured by Friesens in Altona, Manitoba in March, 2023.

Printed using paper from a responsible and sustainable resource,
including a mix of virgin fibres and recycled materials.

Printed and bound in Canada.

DCB Young Readers
An imprint of Cormorant Books Inc.
260 Ishpadinaa (Spadina) Avenue, Suite 502, Tkaronto (Toronto), ON M5T 2E4
www.dcbyoungreaders.com
www.cormorantbooks.com

STANDING ON NEPTUNE

... this is about what happened ...

Except
I've been thinking about the word *happened* —
the way it speaks of events and moments that
have been left in the past, as though,
having taken place, they are
trapped in time gone by.

Which is a peculiar notion when you
think about it. Because the truth is:
everything that *was*
becomes part of
what *is*.

So.

This is my story, but it is not
the story of me — only of
a moment and moments that
took place in my life
and crept into who I am.

... skipping the intros ...

Every story has a main character. In this
one, I have claimed that part as my own.
It is a role you are unlikely to envy.

There are others, of course.
The cast of supporting characters.
Or, actually, and after a
moment's pause,
I will call them
the cast of surrounding characters. But
there is no need for introductions
at the moment. You will only
have forgotten them by the time
they make an appearance.

Although,
there *is* one person you really should
meet before I begin, because after all, this
happening would not have
happened without him.

... Ryan ...

If you're hoping for a magical beginning to the
Brooke and Ryan love story, a saccharine,
"Our eyes met across a crowded room and we just *knew*,"
type of thing, you might as well turn the page now.

It was a decidedly unromantic beginning.

I'd been vaguely aware of Ryan for years.
He was in one of my classes in grade nine, but I can't say
he registered as more than another face in the daily
surge of students hurrying through our school.

Then he happened to sit next to me on the bleachers at a
volleyball game about six months ago. (Okay, it was
April 6, but I only remember the date because it was
my cat Erpo's birthday.) We exchanged
bits of conversation, plus a smile or two if memory serves,
and when the game was over, he made an awkwardly
casual remark that it had been nice talking to me.

And I remember thinking: *Hmmmm.*

After that, there were three or four "chance meetings" at the
cafeteria or lockers where he'd chirp a surprised, "Oh! Hi!"
as if these encounters were organizing themselves.

By the time he made a move, which was to blurt,
"Um, you wanna exchange numbers?" I knew
I was interested. There was something weirdly
appealing about his lack of finesse.

Our first date was a disaster. Agonizing stretches of
dead air, which somehow weren't nearly as painful as
the sudden bursts of conversation.
I wished myself anywhere else, with anyone else.
When it finally ended I could feel his relief
as powerfully as my own. And then —
he kissed me. To this day I'm convinced it was his joy
over the horrid evening *ending* that moved him to
grab my hand and lean in, eyes oddly frantic as he pressed
his lips to mine. But something happened in those seconds,
something —

Well, what do you know.
Apparently there was a bit of magic there after all.

MONDAY

... minus five ...

It happened in a single second in time —
the second when I was
on one knee, tying shoelaces,
through the Monday morning haze of not
one hundred percent alert.

The next moment, I would have headed to school
exactly like any other day
any other beautiful, unremarkable, everyday day.

Except, the radio was on and the announcer's cheery voice
snuck a number past my still-somewhat-sleepy brain
which is when
a minor bit of math nudged its way into
the Ordinary Moment
and time suspended itself.

A simple calculation
that
sucked the air
from my lungs

and turned my feet

to roots.

$x + y = -5$

... which was a figure of speech ...

Of course, feet cannot really
be roots.
I am not a tree.

I am a girl
an unremarkable/
just-like-anybody girl
with a tiny place in the
world.
A place that is/has been
mine alone.

Except a lot can change when
a number
starts to
stomp and shout
in your brain.

... the air I breathe ...

Deep breaths.
That is what my mother used to prescribe
when the small child I once was
held her breath, in moments when she was
very, very hurt or sad or angry
or frightened.

Deep, deep breaths.
As though I can draw in oxygen
until it fills my whole body with
pure, clean air,
inhaling until there is
no room for anything else.

I will be light; I will be transparent.
I imagine myself becoming a balloon
rising and floating away
getting smaller and smaller until I become
a dot, until I disappear
altogether.

... auto-walk ...

I do not recall the walk to school
the trees and roads, their sights and sounds
the people who waved or smiled or spoke
or did not.

My feet move forward, just as they have done
so many times and days, plodding without
regard for the way
my heart is racing.

They move forward
as though this is just
any other stroll
toward tomorrow.

... lost moments ...

Somewhere in the space between
that second and *this* one,
I have fallen out of rhythm. A
pinch of time has vanished, nothing more
than a small collection of seconds
which should hardly be worth
the smallest thought.

But today

Today it is enough to steal away my
morning routine,
smiles and greetings
"hello"
"how are you"
"see you at lunch"

Today, when I so long to
anchor myself in his smile, his voice,
the touch of his hand.

... the substitute ...

My favorite teacher, Mr. Chastain, is

not here today. He has been absent a lot this semester,

which has given rise to rumors of

health issues, or marital problems.

Instead, a new face peers out over the room — a

stranger, perched casually against the edge of

Mr. Chastain's desk. As if it is his.

He does not speak. Not even after both bells have rung.

His strategy is to let his own silence spread through the class until

all is quiet.

When it is apparent this tactic is not working, he

clears his throat, says good morning, asks for our attention,

identifies himself as Mister somebody. I miss the name because

I am busy noticing how awkward the word *Mister* sounds

coming from him.

Finally, he tells us he is subbing for Mr. Chastain.

In case we don't understand how the system works.

And actually, *he* doesn't look like *he* knows

much about Writer's Craft, not like Mr. Chastain, who

makes it seem possible that even I

can create worlds with words.

Mister somebody is young.
It is partly amusing and
partly awkward watching him try to
fit into the teacher role. It puts me in
mind of someone wearing clothes
that are two sizes too large.

None of this is important, except that it
distracts me from the thought frozen in
my brain, at least for part of the period.

... the shape of tension ...

Somehow

seconds turn

to minutes and

minutes to hours

until the morning has

lumbered by with its words

and more words dawdling along

until at last, the noon bell announces

our lunch hour's suspension of learning.

I find him watching, waiting, his face

turned toward me, a smile already

sent ahead to greet me before I

have reached his side. But it

dissolves as the words rise

like bile in my throat, up

into the air, up into his

brain and I see him

grasp their full

meaning.

... questions ...

It does not take long for his
reaction.
"Are you joking?"
he asks.

I can barely keep myself from giving him the look
the one he hates, the one that makes him think
I'm judging his failure to grasp some
some simple point, some obvious
bit of information. Which, if I'm
honest, I have definitely done.

I don't (trust myself to)
answer
while his eyes send out
panic
anger
fear
and find their way, at last, to
hope
and hope wraps itself in a new
question.

It *could* mean something else,

right?

... answers ...

Actually, no.

I am not joking.

I did not get up this morning and

decide it might be

ever so amusing to pretend

my period is

five days

late.

Even though, obviously,

that would be

hilarious.

And I suppose it's true, there are other things

it *could* mean

but the one that matters is the one

that is exploding in my brain —

the one his brain would rather

sidestep than

think about

even though

we both know

it is possible.

... holding back from a bestie ...

I avoid Ryan for the rest of lunch hour, which is
not much of a challenge since he makes
no effort to search me out.
I try to feel smug at the thought
that I've made him too nervous to come to me, but
it's a wretched sort of victory.

I join Emma in the lunchroom and sit,
tucked in with my back against the wall. She knows
the instant she sees my face that something is
wrong and that makes me feel a little less
frightened, a little less alone, for
just a second.

We don't keep things from each other
and I almost tell her.
Emma, Emma — I am so afraid.
The words are there, ready to
                    leap

                        off

                            my

                                tongue.

At the last second, I swallow them down,

shake my head, force a smile, claim a headache,

throwing a lie over the truth like a soft yellow blanket

because

I am remembering last summer. A silly spat,

nothing really. It would have been forgotten

long before now except for the

secret, just a small one, but one

she had sworn to keep,

and yet, somehow, it got out

the very next day.

... first impressions ...

I suppose if this was all you knew, if your
first impression of my very
very best friend was
shadowed by a minor failing, you
could not be blamed for thinking
ill of her. And this

puts me in the odd position of
having to defend my friend from
my own words
(even though those words are true).

But I have also been guilty
of small betrayals.
And in that light, I offer a second
first meeting with
Emma.

... Emma ...

If you have a best friend, you already know elements of who
Emma is to me. If you don't, I can never explain how we
fit into each other's lives.

Even so, something must be said. I will begin by
borrowing words from someone else. A poet, named
William Blake, whose remark I found quoted in among
some forgotten thing I was reading:

"The bird a nest, the spider a web, man friendship."

When I first saw it, I wondered why
this little line had been chosen from all
the many things that have ever been said about
friendship, but —
the more I thought about it,
the bigger it got. So that
before long, these ten simple words had lingered
in some part of me in such a way that
my heart seemed to be nodding yes.

Emma takes that place in my life, the best friend place
a nest, a web, a home of safety and belonging.
There are a thousand reasons why, but even if I
told you every last one, even if you knew that:

Emma listens to things I tell her, listens in a way
that does not make me think she is planning
what to say when I stop speaking.
Or
Emma is strangely proud of the fact that she has never had a
s'more.
"Not once in my whole entire life," she tells people, even though
their reactions are rarely what she may have hoped.
Or
Emma cries at movies, but not when you would expect it,
not when the dog dies or the lover leaves or
other things happen that touch the common heart.
...
I could go on, but no matter how much I say
it cannot be the whole story
because
the story of *her* is not the story of *us* and that is
what friendship is made of.

... acting normal ...

Somehow, there are classes to get through
one moment at a time.

I switch on autopilot,
walk through the halls, in and out of classrooms,
words come and go while I
try to muffle the echo in my head,
five days, five days, five days, five days.

Each class gives me just enough time to
convince myself that
the next stop in the bathroom will bring
a sign that all is well.

Instead, I discover that
hope can be flushed away.

... assignment ...

Ms. Gallagher has spent most of Science class
trying to get us excited about the
solar system, a subject I barely found interesting
when we studied it back in some earlier grade.
And today — especially today, it's hard to imagine
caring about a bunch of planets whose complications
are so very many million light years
beyond my grasp.

I do my best to focus anyway, catching
phrases like, "career targets, earth and space
science," and "goal-oriented curriculum,"
as they glide past me in the air.
Maybe I can divert my thoughts
from the fear clutching me.
A long distance detour
from the world I inhabit.

Ms. Gallagher's eyes light up when she reaches
her BIG announcement.
"I am giving each of you —" and here she pauses,
convinced this builds suspense, excitement, interest,

"*either*, a fascinating career in this field, *or* —
your very own planet!"
Some of my classmates show their
suspense, excitement, interest,
with groans and eye rolls and shoulder slumps.

Normally, I give Ms. Gallagher credit for trying
but not today.
Today all I feel is
impatient
annoyed
afraid
afraid
afraid.

She makes her way around the room, smiling,
holding a plastic food storage dish full of
folded slips of paper.

We each extract one. Between the two choices, I'd prefer
a career. Specifically, something not too complicated.
Instead, I find myself looking at a single word.
Neptune.

I crumple and crush my folded slip of paper into a
very tiny ball
and drop it in the wastebasket on my way
out of class.

Ryan Speaks: One

I guess I handled that in the worst possible way, but, come on. It was like getting nailed by the hardest sucker punch ever.

All I know is I was at my locker when I saw Brooke in the hall, heading my way. I stuck my hand up to wave hello which was when the look on her face registered. She didn't wave back, but even with that, and the way she was coming at me, I had no reason to think there was anything seriously wrong.

To be honest, what I *was* thinking was that, whatever had set her off, she sure looked cute.

"Hey," I said before she quite reached me. I kept smiling too because if Brooke thinks I messed up about something, she'll use my face to convict me. A frown, a hint of worry is as good as a confession to her.

So yeah, even though I could see she was upset, that's what I did. Smiled.

She didn't smile back. She grabbed my arm and leaned in.

"I need to talk to you," she said. "Right now."

We found a corner with no one around, but it took her a couple of minutes to speak.

Meanwhile, I was trying to figure out what she was mad about. Something I did, or maybe something I forgot. I didn't have a clue. All I knew was I was ready to tell her I was sorry. For whatever it was — who cares? I hate fighting. It's better to do what you've gotta do to get it behind you.

She cleared her throat. There were tears building up, but she swiped at them, and then she said it. Words like a fist in the gut.

My period is late. Five days.

I asked if she was joking — a moron's reflex, I admit. It made her furious. I could see that right off, so I tried to think of something to say to calm her. To calm both of us, I guess.

Which is why I pointed out (and it seemed like a perfectly reasonable thing to say) that it could mean other things.

If anything, that made her even madder. She hissed a few words that I didn't register, cut me down with her eyes, turned, and walked away.

I should have, and honestly, I *would* have gone after her, but I was too busy trying not to puke. And before I got my feet to move again, a text came blazing to my phone.

Do not tell ANYONE and don't even THINK about trying to text or talk to me today.

The rest of the day? Everything else? A blur.

... best worst job ever ...

Mom likes to say that it's good for
me, watching my kid brother Kevin after school.
It's teaching me responsibility, which is
pretty convenient for her.

It's usually only two, sometimes three
times a week, and I *do* get paid (not the
going rate for babysitting — I checked)
but it sometimes gets in the way of
other things I'd like
to do.

I don't complain though. Not because I'm a saint
but because Kevin doesn't like after-school
programs. Also, he's not such a bad kid.
I bet you'd like him.

... Kevin ...

(the brother I love and sometimes lock in the laundry room)

My kid brother Kevin, is nine —
eight years my junior. I suspect he was
an accident or
an afterthought.
Mom refuses to confirm or deny either of these theories.

Kevin is joyous in a quirky, lovable way. His smile is real.
He regularly ranks as my
favorite human on the planet because
he does cool things without
realizing they're cool, which I think is
the only time "cool" counts.

When he was six, even without being bribed, Kevin kept quiet
about a china teacup I had knocked to the floor, where it
became china bits. When it was still a cup, it had been our
great-grandmother's.
("Granny" to me and Kevin.)
Back then she had a special cabinet to show off her treasures —
dishes and trinkets passed down from her mom.

Now Granny lives in a care home. She does not
like it there. She refers to it as, "This flapjacketty place."
(Flapjacketty is her version of what she calls cussery.)

Mom reminds Granny that she has her own
bathroom and television and
not a care in the world.
Granny says maybe she *wants* to have
a care in the world.

Hmmmm.
I don't know how my Granny snuck in there. Probably because I
miss her, and wish I'd been more careful with her teacup.
I will now go back to telling you about my brother, Kevin.

Aside from staying quiet about broken dishes and other such
"crimes" (his word) Kevin's virtues include a sometimes astounding
sense of fairness and a peculiar love of spiders, which he will
rescue and "re-home" (also his word) somewhere they can
live out their remaining stitch of time in
harmony with nature.

He's not an angel, of course. When Kevin's mischievous side
breaks loose
it's like being trapped in the dark with a scourge of mosquitoes.

Those are the moments I want to lock him in the
laundry room, which, in case you're wondering,
I *have* done.

Unfortunately, Kevin is getting faster and harder to wrangle
so his days in the laundry room are likely at an end.
I suppose that doesn't matter much since being locked
in there only makes him laugh.

If my parents were forced to pick favorites, I am
ninety percent sure
Mom would claim Kevin and Dad would choose me.
But they both love each of us very much.
Of course. And this was something they
said many, many times a few years ago while
they ripped our world apart.

... the danger of silence ...

I almost regret telling Ryan, "Do not call. Do not
text. Do not come over. Do not even think about
trying to talk to me right now."   Almost.

I still don't want to talk to *him.* Not yet.
But an urge is swelling in me, a need
to speak, to release this mad jumble of thoughts.

I'm fearful that if I try to hold it in, it will
start to rumble and roil until
I will begin to make some simple remark such as
"have you seen the remote?" or
"pass the broccoli, please,"
only to be overtaken by a mad impulse to
shout, "I think I might be pregnant!"

I imagine the horror, the stunned silence that would
fall on me, and worse, the confessions that would
be demanded when the sound comes back on.

There is Emma, of course. If I could just resurrect the
I-can-trust-her-one-hundred-percent-no-matter-what

certainty I used to have. I remind myself that what happened
last summer was a tiny thing by comparison — a scratch that
barely broke the surface. This is not the same.
This would be a knife plunged to the heart.
An unthinkable betrayal.

I decide I have hesitated for nothing. Of course I can —
I *will* trust her. But it is strange, knowing there was a
decision to be made. Because, haven't I always
gone to her whenever a
haven was needed
a nest, a web,
a friend.

She will be my ally, no
matter what. She will stand at my
side and do what she can to keep
the darts from striking me.

... we interrupt this plan to bring you ...

I have composed an "I need to talk to you" text to
Emma and my finger is hovering over *send* when
the sound of Kevin's anger breaks in.

Although, of course, anger itself is not a sound.
What I hear is the stomp of feet, a harshly-closed door,
a sort of undefined lament. It is a combination I recognize,
an echo of experience.
Someone or something has hurt my brother.

I put my phone down and go to his door. Tap, tap, tap. Gently.
"Kev? You okay?"
A pause. Muffled shuffling moves toward me.
His door opens just a crack. Enough to see the flush of
his face. His eyes avoid mine.

"Can I come in?"
He shrugs, but steps back. Permission. I nudge
the door and step inside.
"Want to tell me what's wrong?"
It takes a bit of time. I wait in silence, seated beside him
on the bed. Finally, a story makes a halting start. An

injustice, deeply felt. I put my arm around his shoulders and help him usher it out. There is no solution to offer, but presence and comfort are what he needs most.

This, I can give.

The text message to Emma remains unsent.

... the helpful properties of distraction ...

Strangely, after those moments with
my brother, I feel calmer, and the urge to
tell Emma has passed
for the moment.
It is plain to see that
distraction
could be my greatest
safeguard against
fear and panic
at least until I *know.*

In a mental search of somewhere else to
turn my attention
a crumpled scrap of paper unfolds itself
in my memory. I will begin
investigating my
assigned planet.
Neptune.

... sketching Neptune ...

I am surprised to learn that five centuries ago,
before the planet we call
Neptune was known, before it
had a name, before its status,
substance, and size had been confirmed,
Galileo twice sketched what he believed to be
just another star.

It is not lost on me that Neptune was
there all along, whirling and turning
while Galileo's pencil moved, insensible to
the undiscovered truth.

It is not lost on me that what was
known or unknown,
what had been
seen or unseen,
in no way altered what
was.

... years between ...

Alone in my room, tucked into
the warm cocoon of my bed
my thoughts run oddly to a
comforter I had as a little girl.

Bright, happy flowers boldly waved me
to sleep each night back then. Waved me
to sleep where I dreamed my
magically peaceful little-girl dreams.

And now, here I am, in what feels like the very next
moment, as if the years between those slumbers
and this night are just one more dream,
except, of course, the magic is gone.

Tonight, sleep lurks like an enemy, its dark
eyes mocking me with promises of twisted
sheets and sighs, of troubled dreams.
Of nightmares morning cannot scatter.

TUESDAY

... Tuesday morning ...

This is one of Mom's work-at-home days, which is
unfortunate. When she is needed at the office, she
hurries about, preoccupied, her parental radar
turned to its lowest setting.

This morning, she is sipping coffee, eating toast, and asking
devoted-mother questions. She wants to know if there is
anything new, anything I want to talk about.
Which is why I find myself telling her ...

the first thing my brain grabs and ejects
in a cascade of over-excited babble —
Galileo and star sketches and Neptune.

In spite of my certainty there is no way she
won't notice these weird vibes, Mom seems
unalarmed. Surprised, yes, but in a kind of
pleased way, as if I've just revealed
some unexpected depth of character.

… I suppose it's time you met my parents …

When I think about it, it's a little strange that
I have never
(at least, not in any meaningful way)
introduced my mom and dad. Unless you count,
"This is my mom," or, "This is my dad,"
which I do not.

And even though they take up so much space in
my life, I cannot think of anything to say that doesn't
sound as though I am composing
online dating profiles.

Mom
"Super organized but can still be spontaneous. Big fan of kitchen
gadgets and slip-on shoes. Not a morning person.
Once rescued a nest of baby robins."

Dad
"Tries not to take anything too seriously. Never stops believing his
team will be next to win the Stanley Cup. Loves board games.
Gives up coffee at least five times a year."

And honestly, I'm not sure how much you even need to know
about them, except for this one thing —
the main thing to me, which is that they
aren't married to each other anymore.

I'm almost certain you guessed that already. It
happened when l was twelve. The divorce.
For a while it felt like running down a
wobbly flight of stairs and l remember
how the air seemed thinner.

Eventually,
l learned how to walk and breathe and
live in the new world.
Eventually,
l stopped believing yesterday was
coming back.

I'm fine now, by the way. Adjusted, possibly even well.
Apparently, being told it was not my fault until the very
sound of those words made me cringe
has done no lasting harm.

I live with my mom and spend
every second weekend with my dad, although he
likes to remind me that
they have shared custody.

It was that way for a while.
The "Mom & Dad" couple
split apart, turned into
solo acts: Mom and Dad.
But of course, that changed too.

... sparents ...

After the divorce ... time passed. Then
they came. Step-parents, extras,
like spare parts, which is how I came to
call them sparents.

Dad remarried first. His second wife, Gloria, took me on a
"just us girls" date where we ate ice cream and she
told me solemnly she was not
trying to replace my mother.

I was tempted but did not answer that I, in return,
was not trying to replace her daughter. I expect
that would have seemed ridiculous to her.

Eventually, Gloria stopped trying so hard and I stopped making
fun of her perky smile behind her back.
I have to say I like her
better now than I did when she was in stepmother overdrive.

Mom's new husband, Jerry, the most recent "family"
addition is okay, if a little dull.

I'm expected to let them in, these

people, even though it is not

easy. Not after years of

clutching the remnants

of what was. You can't just

throw your arms open after that.

But I am trying.

So now there are four instead of two

like a cell dividing and doubling

mom minus dad = mom plus "dad" plus "mom" plus dad

divorce's version of mitosis.

... mirror, mirror ...

This talk of family,
who they are,
who they are to me, and,
who they are to each other
has me standing,
looking into the mirror
on my bedroom door.
It is
designed for
a full body look.
Does this outfit work?
Is anything showing that
I would rather hide?

But today, I find
another question. One I have never
in my entire life,
considered.

Who am I?
I am Brooke, of course. But so much
of my identity is tied to

others. I am a
sister, a daughter,
a friend, and a girlfriend,
a teenager, a student.

I can see all of those. I recognize
the words, the smiles and
frowns, the touches and
the many ways my
heart connects
to each.

But
no matter how hard I stare
I cannot begin to see a
mother.

… ready to talk …

The locker area is congested, as usual when
I get to school — on schedule today. There is a
trembling feeling of hope in me while I watch
(without being obvious about it, although doesn't
everyone think they're pulling that off when
in fact, no one ever is?)
for Ryan to appear.

It is all rehearsed in my head, how I will
react when he comes to me, in such a way that he
will know my anger is gone and I am willing to
set aside the words from yesterday.

I picture earnest apologies, clasped hands,
renewed hearts and moist, grateful eyes.
There will be the togetherness of WE.

But when the bell rings and Ryan has not appeared, I
know he has found a reason not to come today.
I swallow my disappointment but not my pride. I will not
let myself text to ask … anything.

... message from a mouse ...

The sub is still filling in for Mr. Chastain.
Today he writes his name on the
board. It is Mr. Smodgeworth, which sounds
to me like a character in a fairy tale.

Someone at the back of the room asks if
he is going to be here all week. This causes
Smodgeworth to launch an answer that sounds
very much like a recital.

"Who knows," he intones. "Who can say what
tomorrow will bring. We cannot see a single
moment into the future. Why, we barely see the
one in which we are living, if truth be told. Nor do we
know what circumstance, large or small may disrupt
the best laid plans of mice and men? And what," he asks with
an eyebrow raised, "do we know of that?"

Of course we know that *Of Mice and Men* is a book and
movie title but we're not prepared to say where
that title came from. There are a few wild
guesses, which seem to pain Smodgeworth.

"I am not asking you to *speculate*," says he,
with a sad shake of his head.

We have, it seems, let him down, but we are eager to
redeem ourselves. To keep the conversation going will
mean a shorter lesson. It also risks more homework,
but we rarely think that far ahead.

So we hear about a poem.
To a Mouse by Robert Burns.
Smodgeworth has us read it and for the rest of the class
we discuss what it means. I find myself wondering if that
was his lesson plan all along.

Mostly, though, I wonder if everything in the sphere of me
is going to shape *it*self to *my*self, like the
lessons in a rhyme from 1785.

... lying to a bestie ...

Emma is watching me. I feel the probing of her
eyes. She has figured out that I am with-
holding something from her, a secret even
though we proudly claim to tell each
other absolutely everything.

When she draws a deeper-than-usual breath, I know
what is coming and I am not wrong. She leans in just
a little and delivers three short sentences, clipped for
efficiency, pointed for effect.

Something is going on with you.
Tell me what it is right now.
And don't lie to me.

I nod. And then I lie to her.
I tell her a one hundred percent made up
story about a big blow-up between my dad and step-mom.
I claim to be worried there could be another divorce. Emma
reaches over, gives my hand a fierce squeeze and reassures
me these things happen and everything will be all right.

"You should have said something," she scolds me.
"That's what friends are for."

I agree that I feel much better and confess to feeling
silly for keeping it from her. "It just seemed too
private," I claim. "Like I shouldn't be
telling anyone else about their business."

Emma understands completely. How silly I was to worry.
And then we spend the rest of lunch hour talking
about this non-existent problem.

I'm left feeling guilty and ashamed, and yet I am
stuck once more in that place, the place where
I cannot find the missing fraction of trust
and this
adds a heavy kind of sadness
to the jumbled heap of my emotions.

... dinner out ...

First thing I notice when I get home from school is
Mom. Specifically, Mom wearing what she calls
one of her "smart" outfits. Plus lipstick.

My fear-charged instincts get right to work
manufacturing bizarre scenarios where I
am cornered, my secret exposed ... until
thankfully, I remember. Jerry's birthday.
Dinner out. I will be instructed to
put on something decent, as if the clothes I wore to
school today were culled from a pile of rags.

Less than an hour later we are seated at a round table in
one of those places where soft orchestra music floats
over the waiter's head. He gives us enticing details about
specials and seems mildly disapproving when we
turn, un-enticed, to our menus.

Jerry's daughter, AKA my "stepling" Mel is on my left.
She's in a twelve-year-old sulk and
working hard at it. A plate of Farfalle with
cream sauce and fresh parm distracts her for a bit, but

she catches herself between bites and remembers to grumble,
"If *I* ever have kids, *I* won't force them to
go places they don't want to go."

It's the kind of remark that may have gone unnoticed,
had her indignation not been in search of an ally.
"*You* would never do that, would you, Brooke?" she
asks in her loudly earnest twelve-year-old voice.
"I mean, if you ever had a kid."

I am afraid to speak, afraid a single word will betray me, but I
am saved by Mom, who leans in to remind Mel
it is her father's birthday and she ought to make
make more of an effort.

Mel resumes her sulk while I exhale.

... unexpected crack ...

Mom has just turned onto
our street and Jerry is saying what a nice treat it
was to have everyone together to celebrate his birthday
when something swells up inside me, a flood of emotion
unexpected, in a nothing moment — like a
volcano erupting without warning

Somehow,
I don't quite
know how, I make
it inside before the rush
of tears spills out, coursing
down my cheeks, falling to
my chest where they soak into
the fabric covering my heart,
and are halted there by a
mere cotton-polyester
blend

... giveaway ...

Never let anyone persuade you that a splash of
cold water can entirely hide the evidence of
tears. That is a lie. There is something that lingers in
eyes that have just wept — a mournful
whisper of sadness that cannot be disguised.

I am persuaded that Mom will catch this, and
ask questions. As a cover, I fake sneeze loudly
several times before emerging
into the hallway.

But worse than anything is that I can't be sure the outburst is
really over. It feels close to the surface, cheated
out of its full release. I know it could return at
any moment — that the threat will be there, hovering
until it has been properly cried out.

It is lucky then, that Neptune awaits, my planet and for
that moment, my rescuer. No one disturbs a girl
closed in her room, working on a school assignment.

... visitor ...

A closed door is no match for Erpo the cat, not when he
is determined to gain entry. There is insistent meowing, just
outside my room — the kind of feline lament that suggests great
suffering is going on. He accompanies himself, like a
one-cat-band, with pawing and tapping, until I can
no longer resist.

When I open the door, Erpo is suddenly undecided. I wait until
he strolls in, head high. He crosses to the bed without
so much as a me-ward glance. Having been forced
to beg, he must now shun me until sufficient
fawning and acts of devotion have taken place.

You might be wondering about the name. Erpo. That is
thanks to Kevin, who couldn't pronounce the
name Erpo had when we got him from the shelter.
Funny, I can't even remember what that name was.

When I have appeased him, I return to my desk, and to my
planet. But the oddest thing! Erpo, who loves curling up on my
folded spare blanket, leaves his place of comfort. He lands
on the desk, startling me, and remains there while I work.

... how Johann Gottfried Galle started a fight ...

To attend this dispute, we must take ourselves
back to 1846 and that moment when
Johann Gottfried Galle found what had previously
appeared only as a star in Galileo's sketch. And we might
expect, having been first to sight this brand new
planet, Galle would be credited with the find.

But here's the part where math steps in, because
before Galle came along, two fine gents,
French mathematician Urbain Le Verrier and
English mathematician John Couch Adams,
independently of each other, had predicted the
presence of Planet X, which we know as Neptune,
in that precise spot in the faraway sky.

An argument ensued. Of course it did. Both chaps and their
countries insisted theirs was the strongest claim but no
winner could be agreed upon and today, the credit
is equally shared between the two.

What catches my attention over every other detail
in the discovery of Neptune

is that this planet was

first detected,

not through a telescope,

but *mathematically*

reminding me that yesterday's

calculation requires an

update, because now

x + y = −6

WEDNESDAY

... footwear woes ...

Denise Landry's new shoes may be
ruined — dreadful news that reaches me as
I rummage in my locker before class.
Whatever Denise and her shoes stepped
in has made a blotch. A dark blotch that
could be some kind of oil or perhaps
(pause to shudder) something even worse.

Denise loves those shoes. She loves them so much
and her mother is going to kill her if she has
ruined them on practically the first day
she ever wore them.

Several of Denise's friends have created a kind of
emotional support wall around her and I hear
suggestions of how she may yet overcome this
tragic happening and go on with her life.

I close my locker and head to
class trying not to let it bother me that
there is still no sign of Ryan.

... Gallagher's galaxy ...

Ms. Gallagher is looking for volunteers
because — dramatic pause — we are
going to build a planetary gallery and
IF we do a really good job, an amazing job, we
will have a feature page in the yearbook. She has
already worked this out with the yearbook committee.

Kim and Davey and Stu always volunteer for this kind of thing.
"We can meet at my place," Davey says,
an announcement he makes every time. Their love of
extra credit or whatever it is that motivates them lets
the rest of us off the hook.

Except, today a fourth hand appears in the air and that hand is
mine. I tell myself maybe fate will reward my good deed, but
that is not really why I have stepped up. I will just pretend
it is and see if I can fool myself.

... misunderstood ...

My heart leaps as I catch a glimpse of
Ryan on the way to my next class. His face
looks ghostly, moving through the corridor,
eyes darting this way and that. It isn't until
they shift in my direction, find me, and stop
scanning that I realize it is
me they are seeking.

A rush of joy comes and in that
second I know I have been longing
to see him, to talk this through,
to lay my head against his chest and feel
his arms holding me close
to his heartbeat.

Except, something in his expression is ...
wrong. In a flash it
registers that he was, in fact, not
seeking, but *watching* —
guarded, distrustful,
apprehensive.

My heart sinks, gladness crumbles.
If only I could catch his eye, find a
way to reassure him, to let him know
with a smile or wave how very much I
want us to be okay. But there is no
chance. He passes by without
wavering, his face set like granite,
forward-facing and cold.

... the lost class ...

I barely know what class I am in next,
fighting misery while words
bounce off the walls around me,
while classmates do the everyday things, the
silly and flirty and defiant things that
give them voices when they are
expected to be silent.

I struggle past the thought that I cannot
breathe, that my chest is squeezed so
tight that air cannot gain entry.
A sense of panic has made my
pulse race and my heart pound.

Slow deep breaths eventually calm the
wild rush of dread so that
by the end of class I have talked myself
into a corner of hope, a geometric crook where
what will be is governed by what is desired.

... and still I cannot ...

Emma's eyes are lit with excitement when I
slide into place for lunch. Without a word, she
reaches into her bag, pulls out a bento box, and
shoves it across the table.

I pry the lid open and find a slab of pound cake,
a specialty at Emma's house. The scent of lemon
teases my nose.

"Mom and I made it last night," she tells me.
"Because you've been sad, and I know
how much you love this."

My eyes fill with tears while my conscience
condemns my lies and mocks the fears that
keep me from telling her the truth.

In that moment, it seems certain her kindness
has broken through, that the words must come.
But when I speak, it is only, after all, to
offer a trembling thanks.

... what happens when you volunteer ...

Stu catches me on the way to my last class of
the afternoon. For a few seconds I cannot
grasp what he's saying, not because his words are
unclear, but because I had almost forgotten about
the galaxy I said I would help create.

The team is eager to get started, he tells me.
Can I meet them at Davey's place after school
tomorrow for a bit of *brainstorming*?

I keep from smiling (because I have never heard
a student use that word before) as he gives me
Davey's address. Which just happens to be where the
truth of why I volunteered can be found.

According to the hurrying-off-to-class Stu, this is
going to be awesome.

... suspicious eyes ...

It was only about a year ago that I realized we all
observe our surroundings in different ways —
what a person notices, or the details that slide past, how well
each of us recalls faces and colors and so many other things.

My brother Kevin is a peculiar combination: hyper-alert to
some things, totally oblivious to others. Today, I become
the subject of his scrutiny in a way that unnerves me
probably because — and maybe you have felt this at some
time — when you have a very large secret, it seems impossible
that it can be truly and entirely hidden.

I check my history twice, although I am sure I cleared it
after every search that might betray me. But might there
have been a moment when I'd left my room, a
moment when he could have wandered in and seen:
"teenage pregnancy" or "early symptoms of pregnancy?"

My brain gets busy producing questions I cannot answer.
I doubt Kevin would say anything to Mom, but
would he ask me about it? And if he did,
what would I tell him?

I wonder, for the first time, what exactly he knows
about the facts of life. My face flames at the
thought — my little brother suddenly grasping the
truth of how such a thing could have happened.

And then, just as I'm trying to slow-breathe away my
panic, he asks if anything's wrong. Specifically: am I sick?
"You know what? I *have* been feeling a little off," I say.
"Probably picked up a bug somewhere."

It is getting harder to carry the
weight of the lies I have
told this week.

... other explanations ...

The sight and smell of dinner,
proudly prepared by Jerry,
sits like a warm heap
of sludge on my plate.

I usually like this dish, a casserole of sorts
with rice and cauliflower and bits of chicken.
But today, the scent wafts up and sticks like
a gag in the back of my throat.

Somehow, I manage to eat just enough to avoid suspicion,
taking tiny bites with sips of water, drawing in slow,
careful breaths. I pretend Kevin is not watching me and am
grateful when Mom distracts him with a funny story from
her day.

When the table has been cleared and the dishwasher
loaded, I retreat to my room where I assemble
an impressive list of *other* reasons I may be
feeling queasy.

... another episode of ...

Once again I
am lying on my
bed, except
this time there
are no tears or
long despairing
shudders.
This time
there is a
frozen knot of
empty — filling
me.

Eventually, I
I manage to
force my
thoughts
outward and
upward
to the
skies.

... probing Neptune ...

This planet, bestowed on me by means of a
scrap of paper, has turned out to be a
gift of sorts, drawing me away
from earth and self.

There is a feeling of almost-magic, imagining this vast and
frozen ball of brilliant blue, spinning alone
three billion miles from the Sun
set apart by time and space.

How little we must truly know, in spite of our
mathematicians and interstellar missions —
such as the astounding journey made by
space probe Voyager 2. I envision it
rushing through outer space for twelve patient
years, in order to pass nearby, a tourist
on a record-breaking photo shoot.

We have only seen its surface, felt awe
and wonder as it performs its dual act,
that endless commotion of motion,
rotating even as it revolves, traveling steadily

around the sun — an odyssey achieved
in a mere hundred and sixty-five years.

How very much more there must be,
beneath the blue,
beyond the great and dark divide
of this galaxy, which is itself
but a speck, a mere spot of dust
in infinity.

Our shared truth, I suspect, is that
it too has secrets, hidden beneath
what can be seen.

... holding it together while buying fruit ...

Mom calls me from my room to go with her to the
grocery store. She passes me a cluster of mesh bags and
sends me to pick out fruit. I'm looking over apples when
a message comes in from Ryan.

I know you're still mad but we should talk. Really,
there was just that one dumb mistake so
what are the odds

I read it twice, shove my phone into my pocket and pick out
four apples to join the bananas, plums, and pineapple
in my cart.
Another ping comes.

Come on please

Should I grab some berries too? I decide instead to
add a small bunch of green grapes to what I've gathered.

Can you just answer

I stab-compose an angry reply.

You want me to reassure you, is that it?

Hold your hand? Tell you everything will

be all right? You really think YOU'RE the one

who needs support right now?

My finger hovers over SEND but I

think better of it. He's scared too — I get that

and besides, even though his messages aren't exactly

helpful, he *is* reaching out.

Plus I really want to see him.

So I erase what's there and send him a single line.

                    Meet me at our tree in an hour.

... our tree ...

our tree is in

a very small park at

the halfway-between-our-houses

mark. It has a bench where we stopped one

day to talk and drink the hot chocolate I had

brought along because filling the thermos

seemed somehow romantic. We stayed,

talking and laughing and learning

some new things about each

other, until he

leaned in

for just

one kiss

and our

mouths

tarried

while he

gathered

courage

to say the

three words

that made it real

Ryan Speaks: Two

So after three days of silence and hostile looks, when Brooke finally agrees to meet and talk, she picks what she calls our tree. When she started calling it that I had no clue what she was talking about, but I eventually figured out it was the first place I told her I loved her. She keeps track of stuff like that.

I wasn't sure what the point of it was. Going there today I mean. It could have been a good sign, or it could have been bad. I didn't exactly see this as a subject that called for any kind of romantic setting.

But it started out okay. She looked really lost and scared sitting on that bench. When I sat down and put my arm around her, she grabbed me and started bawling. I let her get it out and then when she was wiping her face on her sleeve, I said she was probably worrying for nothing. She didn't answer.

Then I made what I thought was a sensible suggestion. She should get a test as soon as possible, find out for sure, so she can do whatever she has to do next. But for some reason, Brooke didn't like that. She pulled away and moved down the bench enough to put a good six inches between us.

She sat there without saying anything for what felt like a long time. I got the weird feeling I'd walked into some kind of trap, but then I thought about what I'd just said and I saw where I'd made a mistake.

So I let her know I didn't mean she'd be taking care of it by herself. I promised I was going to be with her every step of the way if it turned out it wasn't just a false alarm. Which I still think it probably is.

Brooke started crying again, which was also when she decided to talk. I found it hard to follow, with the sobs and sniffs and weird crying voice and jumbled words coming out of her, but the thing that did get through to me was, she was definitely not looking at this whole situation the way I was. She was ranting about not wanting to have to decide anything and some weird story about a dog biscuit and on and on.

A dog biscuit. Seriously.

I'd stopped hearing her by then because there was a sort of roar in my ears like something whooshing and it was dawning on me that this could turn out to be bad. Real bad.

I mean, we're *seventeen* years old. We're not even out of high school, never mind whatever we do afterward. *What* is she thinking?

So then it turned into an argument, an ugly one. A lot of things got said. She was acting like I should back off, as if none of this had anything to do with me and meanwhile, I was trying to make her see that if she got all stubborn or whatever it could ruin my life, *both* of our lives really, in a big way.

It was obvious she wasn't listening — wasn't going to listen, which made me really mad. I got up to leave. Even started to walk away, but it was like I could feel her, there behind me on the bench, sitting all by herself, so I went back and sat down for a couple of minutes. Neither one of us said anything then, and I knew there was no getting through to her today, so when I felt calm enough to not sound harsh, I told her "Sorry," and then I left.

... the weight of a pup treat ...

Four years ago when I was thirteen and should have
known better, I did something horrible. It was
supposed to be funny at the time.
To me.

I had a teacher I really, seriously did not like. It seemed
nothing was ever good enough for her and I had the
idea back then that she enjoyed being hard on us. Which,
I now see in a different light, but anyway ...

Not long before the winter break, I failed an assignment. (At the
time I would have said *she* failed me.) And I was furious
(at her, of course) enough to let my mind wander to thoughts
of revenge. Eventually those thoughts turned into a plan.

I "borrowed" a dog biscuit at Emma's place, put it
in a small box, and gift-wrapped it.
On the last day before the break, I slipped into the
classroom at noon when no one was around
and left it on her desk.

After lunch, I watched gleefully as the teacher entered the

room and crossed to her desk where the "gift"

quickly caught her eye. For a second or two she

stared, as though she couldn't quite believe what she

was seeing. Then she picked it up and turned it all around.

As her face flushed with surprise and delight, a feeling of

unease took hold of me. She said, "Thank you, whoever left this

anonymous gift." Her voice was soft and warm. She put the box

down and went about teaching, but her eyes

returned to it now and then and they smiled.

She didn't open the box in class, but I have imagined

a thousand times

how it was when she saw what was inside. I picture

how foolish and hurt

she must have felt, to have been taken in by this

act of cruelty, disguised as a kindness.

As I said, four years have passed since then. And I have not yet

freed myself from the memory, its shame and

regret, although believe me,

I have tried.

... night time ...

I cannot sleep.
Not with this anger pulsing through me.

The ugly image of his face,
suspended in my brain, like a holograph,
long after the argument ended.

Like a song set to repeat, it plays and plays.
A flood of hot words spraying me
angry words, and accusing
as though I have done something wrong
I alone, and now I stand
blocking his way
With my sneaky, stupid, stubborn
self
And my refusal to promise that I
(not *we* — that has disappeared, if in fact, it ever was)
will not mess things up
for him.

And later, after all of that
after tears and sobs have

turned to silent fury

he has the nerve to offer

(this galls the most)

a sullen, muttered,

"Sorry."

THURSDAY

... what he didn't/wouldn't hear ...

The thing Ryan doesn't get, is that I cannot make myself
think about this. I've tried, but it's like
hitting a wall.

That must sound strange, since obviously I'm
thinking about it constantly — wondering, scared,
wondering, scared,
wondering,
scared.

But I cannot and am not even going to
try to think about what
will come after. After there is
certainty ... one way or the other.

He speaks as though there is a reset
button and he cannot
fathom why I
will not simply
poise my finger to
push it.

So. After the accusations,
after the insults and anger
the mottled face too close to
mine, after a pillow soaked in tears,
after a morning of feeling broken,
after all that —
a text.

Before I can read the words I must
get past his row of sad emoticons without
throwing my phone. I barely
manage it, and this is my reward:

Really really sorry babe I just feel
cornered I know you must too and
it kind of exploded but you know I
care about you and just want things
to be ok for both of us.

I cannot stop staring at the word he has
chosen to remind me of the enormous
depth of his affection. Not the

love he swore to   then

not a hint of that.

Apparently, he

"cares" for me   now.

... galactic obligation ...

I ache through the next class and almost snap at
Stu when he reminds me of the galaxy thing at
Davey's place after school.
My conscience wants me to back out because *I* know
my true motive, but I just nod.

Kim is on the doorstep when I get there.
"Reporting for volunteer duty," I say.
She puts on a smile and stabs at the
buzzer with her fingertip.

It's only when we are admitted that
her smile morphs into the real thing.
Perhaps volunteering is not the
only attraction for her.

On the other hand, perhaps I
should not be pondering someone *else's*
ulterior motives.

The fact is — Davey has a twin sister. I
barely know her, but

there is one large detail of her life that
never interested me one scintilla, until
now.

Last year she dropped out
of school and it wasn't long
before we all knew why.

The stroller in the hall makes me
blush. To think this is what I have become —
a person who will "volunteer" in order
to spy on someone else's life.

So it serves me right, when the young mom and
baby boy make a brief appearance
and I realize how silly the idea was that I might
gain some insight, an osmosis of sorts, from the
experiences of a person I barely know.

But on the plus side, working on the galaxy with
Stu and Kim and Davey is surprisingly enjoyable.

... the path I've planned ...

Graduation inches closer every day and
there's a file in my brain where
what comes next
is all neatly organized.

The best-case scenario
stretches out in my tomorrow vision
a path where I
will gather up the threads of
wisdom and knowledge
weaving them into the fabric that creates
my place in the world.

They will become part of other bonds —
lifelong friendships forged in
study halls and coffee shops
as we prepare for
our lives.

It has never once occurred to me
that this tapestry-in-waiting could
come unraveled before it's begun.

... patience or ...

A few years ago, an English teacher gave the class a
writing assignment about family connections.
I wrote mine about all the ways Erpo and I are
alike. It began as a joke, a few lines of
messing around before I'd delete the
nonsense and get on with it properly but — oddly
it transformed into something tender and true. I
took a chance and turned it in.

It's here somewhere, among other scraps saved from my
school years. I don't remember a lot of it in detail, but one
shared trait I recall citing was patience. Erpo, being a cat, is
patient by nature, and I thought the same was true for me.
Except, now I'm not so sure. I begin to wonder if
that is merely something I tell myself when I'm slow to
select a course, form a point of view, choose a gift.

Perhaps I am simply frozen in place, afraid of
facing things, of
getting it wrong.

... transformations ...

It's funny how years passed with Ryan occupying the same
spaces as me — school, sporting venues, community, so many
months when he was there, moving around in the periphery of
my life and not one single time did I have *any* kind of
reaction when he passed through my world.
I mean, nada.

And somehow, I went from one hundred percent
indifference all the way to heart-thumping,
tummy-lurching, butterfly bursts of total thrill at
the mere sight of him doing something as dull as
walking, as uninspiring as lifting a hand to wave or
(heaven help me) as simple as flashing an unexpected smile.

And now?

There are moments still when I could whisper promises
of always, trace the lines of his face with my fingertips,
when I long to let my lips linger on his and feel that burst
of happy shivering through me.
Flashes of a peculiar, mournful hope.

But other yearnings are forcing their way to the front,
and in those moments, I wish I could undo every
touch, scrub the memory of his kiss from my lips, purge
him from my heart, and reclaim the freedom that came
with indifference.

Because then,
I could
sidestep
all of this.

... the echo of the unsaid ...

Now that it is much too late to change
anything, I listen for it over and over — the
sound of my own voice and the one
word that could (should) have
prevented this possibility

and I cannot help but wonder, where was
that word? It found its way to my lips more
than once in the past, when, in
wiser moments
I told him   stop.

In the ticking of time before it happened
why did I fail to give voice to it — that
single syllable of great power?

It chills me to think how little it would
have taken, a whisper, a murmur —
how all of this could have been undone
by the sound of one small utterance.

It is pointless, I suppose, to
revisit what cannot be reversed.
We share the choice we made and yet
the burden feels so much my own
because if I am honest, in that
moment I simply
did not *want* to
stop.

... predictions of parental proportions ...

Of all the paths my thoughts have traveled since
Monday morning, there's one place they keep taking me to.
The place with the faces
that will have to be faced
if: Yes.

I try not to imagine it
the day and hour and moment
or how it will create
a break in time
a forever line
between before and after.

I can choose: When
But I cannot choose: If

They will say:
How could you have been so
foolish
irresponsible
reckless
unthinking?

While my silence answers:
I don't know
I don't know
I don't know
I don't know.

They might even ask:
Where did we go wrong?
But that will be
strictly
rhetorical, which is
the way of most
blame-claiming questions.

... bones ...

Like a bystander in my own life, a
witness who can neither look nor
look away, I am drawn to discover what I
do not want to know.

I have learned, for example, in this
reluctant quest, that the bones
in a human body number 270 at birth
but only 206 in adulthood.

At this moment, however, there is an odd comfort in
knowing these numbers do not apply.
Whatever may or may not be hidden within,
research reassures me that I am
not yet
the guardian of bones.

... even though no one's checking ...

My mother is not the type to snoop
although she did once tell me if she ever
had a genuine reason for concern all
bets were off. I'm pretty sure she was talking about
drugs though, and anyway, what can be
uncovered, discovered when there
is nothing more to find than
a state of uncertainty?

Kevin, on the other hand, has never been
strongly inclined to mind his own business
and I know, since his question the other day, that he
senses something — and is curious (determined even) to
find out what that something is.

And so, I clear my browser after
every single search, and walk around
with the tension of one awaiting
interrogation.

... who I am ...

I had the most peculiar thought only moments ago.
A question really.
Am I the same person I would have been at this
moment in my life, if none of this had happened?

It made me very still, as though the slightest
movement might prevent me
from discovering the answer.

Suppose it turns out this was just one of those things, suppose it
sorts itself out, that I am freed from the necessity of facing
whatever must be faced. Suppose that. That cannot undo
the thoughts and feelings that have tumbled through me since
Monday morning.

Even if this is nothing,
it is something. A happening that
is fused and joined to me forever.

... a path to — ...

I keep thinking of the day we took a walk, like toddlers scampering
through a field of daisies under blue skies and
yellow sun. It dazzled our senses and poured
wonder into us until it overflowed.

Somehow, in that brief and beautiful spell,
it seemed we stood on solid ground, a place
of Ever and Forever, where we cast but a single
shadow over the landscape.

But there was no Ever and Forever. I see
that now. The ground has shifted, and all of it,
the petals and sunshine and joy, have
drifted and drained away.

My heart mocks me, counting off
the mere fractures of time it took, from beat to
beat, measuring the distance between
nothing to everything and back.

... my friend Neptune ...

I wonder if anyone else on this planet has ever
had the urge to write a thank you note
to another planet? Perhaps I am first.
Through this week's misery, Neptune has been
the exact diversion I needed.

I have been staring at this
beautiful, brilliant blue ball —
via a photo of course, but facts and
figures dance in my brain behind the image.

Winds of up to 2,100 kilometers/1,300 miles an hour!
Temperatures as low as −221°C / −366°F!
The smallest but the densest of the gas planets.
The more I learn, the more fascinating it seems.
And the further away.

... Triton ...

It's always oddly surprising to me to hear of
the moons of other planets, as though Earth
alone can command an orbiter.

But one of Neptune's moons has captured
my interest. Its largest moon, Triton, is a
bit of an oddity because it moves in a retrograde orbit,
a rotation opposite to the other moons circling the blue ball.
For reasons beyond my grasp, this suggests
Triton was captured by Neptune.

But that isn't all. Triton is slowly, slowly spiraling
toward Neptune and scientists believe gravitational
forces will someday tear it apart, turning it into a massive
ring that will ultimately be drawn in until it crashes
into the planet. Which seems to me a bit of a betrayal,
until it gives rise to the thought that, perhaps,
if a planet had a heart, beating in a secret, hidden
place, then it might be that Neptune sometimes feels
terribly alone?

... standing on Neptune ...

there is

something incredibly

cold and lonely about moving

through the days carrying thoughts and

feelings that cannot be shared, cannot be spoken

of — it is like being frozen in time, suspended far from

my own world ... it feels as though my body has taken

up residence in another part of the universe: the

coldest, farthest place known to mankind,

in a void so vast that I might as well

be standing on

Neptune.

... isn't it odd ...

No matter how
tired you are, or
how desperately you
long for sleep, even
in those moments
a single thought or
an idle question
can jolt your
brain into high
alert.

Such as:
exactly how does
a person go about
choosing
a name
for another
human
being?

... before I was me ...

When I was little, it charmed me to hear
how it took my parents more than three weeks
to settle on my name.

I loved to coax it from my mother, the story of how
twenty-three undecided days passed by.
Days when they tried out and discarded
Sheila, Barbara, Diane and
two variations of Elizabeth
which means, I suppose
that I have been each of these, in turn.

Mom claims Brooke was her idea;
Dad is ninety percent certain he suggested it first.
Either way, it was The One. The matter was
decided and a name was mine at last.
Brooke Morgan Wells.

And I am certain, in those happier times
this name was chosen with great
deliberation and love. The name
of a wanted child.

FRIDAY

... guardian ...

In gym class this morning, a
volleyball
flies toward me and
my hand,
like some confused defender,
rushes to
shield and protect.

It is the not the first time
I have caught these errant digits
acting on their own.
By times I find them
hovering, offering the
gentle caress of fingertips
like they are stroking a kitten.

Baffling gestures
contradicted
by the stone
of my heart.

... the thing with feathers ...

Ms. Gallagher nods at the pages I add to the
pile of assignments on her desk. She cannot begin to
guess how it has helped carry me through
the week. Neptune.

But no. Not a week, actually. Not seven
days. Just the short stretch since Monday
morning.

A tiny span of days made larger by
the size of its moments.

My stomach clenches at the thought of
the promise I made to myself. If
there is no change by tomorrow,
I will face whatever truth is mine.

The juggling of hope and fear must end — and this
may be the last day of hope. The thing with
feathers, according to Emily D.

... out of the blue ...

A memory has crept in, as memories will,
a random intrusion, a moment in life from years ago
crossing through time until its colors and feelings poke
their way into the right now.

There were three of us, small friends at the playground
and, of course, a mother in attendance, seated on the
parent bench with her water bottle and sunglasses
which may be why I cannot see her face or recall
which child she belonged to.

We were cavorting on a set of monkey bars until
somewhere on the way down, I captured a
sliver of wood in the fleshy pad of my palm.
It was a good size and I hollered, but that may have been
nothing more than indignation, since
I cannot recall it hurting.

The mother beckoned me over (*my* mother would have
rushed to the side of a child who had just cried out,
whether or not that child was her own) and decided
I must be escorted home.

I had a fear of splinters back then, a fear that was less about
having one than about having it extracted. It seemed a great
victory when the supervising mom watched me go
inside but did not stay to alert whichever of my
parents was there that day.

For a day or so I harbored this bit of wood, like a
guest who was not to be disturbed, other than by my own
prodding and poking and squeezing. It was this
growing obsession that was my undoing when, in a
moment of absorption, I did not notice my father
approaching.

A very short time later, fine tweezers had tugged it
free, rubbing alcohol had been applied and a lecture
had been dispensed.

I understood even then, as reluctant as I had been, that
it would have been folly to wait for
it to fester and swell and fill with poison.
Just as it would be folly to do that now.

Ryan Speaks: Three

So, just like that, she dumped me. Caught up with me at the end of the day, dragged me into an empty class and said there was no point in us thinking we were going to stay together — not after this. First she "reminded me" about the dog biscuit. And then she told me a random story about a splinter and seemed to expect me to understand what *that* had to do with us. I seriously have no idea what she's talking about when she drags out these bizarre stories.

I didn't even ask. And I didn't say much back, since everything I've said this week has basically been the wrong thing as far as she's concerned.

But I'm not too worried. She just needs some space right now because of being so stressed. I get that.

And I know one thing, I'll never take another stupid chance no matter what. Just thinking about what happened is probably what messed up her system. When she stops worrying herself sick I bet everything will be okay.

She told me, before our fight the other night, that she's going to get a test Saturday, which is tomorrow. Last thing she said to me today was, "I'll let you know what I find out," which made my gut twist.

When this whole mess is over with and things get back to normal, I think we'll be okay. We mostly get along pretty good and I never liked anyone as much as I like Brooke, but the drama this week has been brutal.

... what I saw when I looked in his eyes ...

I can't pretend it was what I wanted
at all. Until this week, I believed Ryan
was a nearly perfect boyfriend.
For me anyway.

But this week has shown me someone I had no wish to see.
The Ryan of these few days is not the person
I've been walking beside all these months.

For a moment, I considered waiting until
tomorrow, until I am holding
an answer in my hand, except,
if it's good news, the relief might
change my mind, especially if my
heart gets into the argument.

And no matter how lost and heartbroken I feel
right now, there could never be any point in trying
to carry on as if we could erase the
awful from the past few days. As if we
could control the echoes.

I thought he might try to talk me into staying
together. But that is just one of many things
I have been wrong about.

It feels as though this entire week
has been a gathering
of regrets.

... speaking of regret ...

The thing about regret
the thing that makes it
so incredibly hard to escape
is that it is your own
voice shouting
accusations, and
mocking you if
you try to justify
or excuse what you
have done.

The thing about regret
is that you can never
ever undo that thing
whatever it is,
that haunts you
and you can never escape
knowing there was a
moment in time when you
could have chosen
otherwise, but
did not.

... oh for a crystal ball ...

For the record, I am
not a coward
even though
I *am* afraid.

What I fear the most is the thought
of taking a step that can
never be undone, knowing it
will shape not only my
future but *me*.

All week it has hovered in my thoughts,
that whatever comes,
I cannot, must not
be persuaded by
fear or
panic or
shame or
desperation.

But the worst thing, the hardest thing
is that there is no way to

anticipate

what a backward

glance from

some time and

place yet to come,

may reveal

has been strewn

along the

way.

... at Dad's ...

Kevin is my alert system for weekends at Dad's.
On those Fridays, he beelines to his room as soon as
we get in the door, digs out his backpack and stuffs in
random articles of clothing. Unlike Mom, Dad doesn't
care if he's "dressed like a vagabond" when we go
to a movie or restaurant or park, so his packing choices
are never an issue.

Dinner tonight is pizza, a relaxed meal on paper plates. Kevin
takes his to the TV room while Dad asks me what's new
since my last visit. I tell him, "Nothing much."
I hope that might still be true.

In the middle of my second slice, I find myself wishing I
was home, with Mom. A weird feeling considering I
have spent the last few days trying to avoid her. And in case
you think maybe the urge has come over me to tell her
everything, that is absolutely not the reason.

The odd thought occurs to me that I feel safer there.
With my mother. I don't know why those words pop
into my head. I am perfectly safe here.

SATURDAY

... on waking ...

Lying in my bed,
awake but unmoving
while bits of time tick by
and my thoughts drift to
what this day will bring
mental images
if yes/if no.

Sleep last night was an
off and on thing — a fickle friend,
not at all surprising under the
circumstances.

A small fist taps at my door,
"Are you up, Brooke?"
Kevin, waiting to be invited
in — a moment later he is sitting
on the edge of the bed, talking
about his plans for the day.
I see how he is watching me
(still watching me) and I am ready when
he interrupts himself to blurt out
what he really came to say.

Something is different, something is
wrong and he is certain I am hiding
a terrible secret.
There is fear in his eyes.

What an incredible kid, this small person I am
blessed to call my brother.

I sit up, prop the pillow behind me.
I look him straight in the eye, unwavering.
I tell him he is right and he is amazing.
I tell him I made a foolish mistake and it is
bothering me, but that it will all be okay.

His voice trembles with the effort to corral his
heart as he exhales the words,
"So, you're not dying or anything."
And then, the longest, tightest hug in history.

... at the bus stop ...

It takes me in without protest, this
small transparent shelter where
strangers gather and wait
to go about their lives.

I am new to this stop, this route.
It is easy to pick out the regulars. There is
something in the way they step inside, sit or
stand — something that says they are
well acquainted with its tired bench.

I tell myself this bus ride is nothing more than
a simple errand, but that is a lie.
In the strangest way, I am about to walk
in Johann Gottfried Galle's shoes, although
what I discover today will only impact
those moving in my own, tiny orbit.

... the purchase ...

I had some vague and mistaken notion
that I needed to ask the pharmacist
for the item I have come to buy.
She tells me that is not the case and points
me to the shelf where they are in plain
sight. As she does, I can see her assessing
my age, perhaps wondering why I have
put myself in this place. Not the store,
but the place in my life where I have taken
a bus across the city in order to keep my
secret as long as possible. Of course,
the pharmacist does not know that it is
my imagination alone that gives rise to
the notion that I have suddenly become
transparent — and that every stranger
I meet can see the question in my
eyes and the tremble in my heart.

... the realization ...

A strange calm comes over me on the
bus ride back. There is a kind of summoning within,
a swelling of strength — courage gathering and
closing around my fear.
I think of how cold and lonely and
alone I have felt at times this week.

This unfamiliar route, surrounded
by a bus full of strangers suddenly seems like
an errand someone else is on. As though it
has nothing to do with me.

My life is not made up of unknowns;
it is a bounty of love, of people who will
be there. No matter how unhappy,
dismayed, or disappointed they may be,
none of that will alter this simple truth:
they will stand with and by me.

Now, so near to "the moment of discovery"
I find myself laughing (which draws a few stares) at
the thought that in this unexpected

journey toward myself
I have borne the weight
of a load others would have shared.

My mother. When have I not been able
to depend on her? My father. What would
make him turn away from me? My brother.
Whose heart has touched me in moments
when I needed it most.

My family. In any
form or shape, is
still as solid as the
Earth beneath my feet.

All the same,
I cannot help but think
this week has
acquainted me with truths
that may only
have been found in the
silence of a solitary path.

... the test ...

Back at my dad's I slip off to my room knowing

all this secrecy, the hiding of

what is possible must end today if —

possible becomes *positive*.

The instructions are simple and I slide

the white plastic stick from its

wrap and tuck it under my waistband,

pulling my hoodie over top and taking

a careful look in the mirror to be sure

nothing shows.

Small delays complete,

I step softly down the hall and slip

into the bathroom.

The thought of what I am about to

learn makes my knees tremble. I take

deep breaths until they steady.

The thought of my parents and how they will

react (if) breaks in — I shut it out just as

quickly. This is not the moment to let

myself be unnerved by assumptions. It
is the time to know and face what
comes next if indeed the thing that may
be is the thing that is.

The girl in the mirror blinks and I see
tears gathering, as though they can wash out the
disappointment of being in
this moment. But then, a
whisper rises from my lips,
steadies my heart, and reminds me
I am not alone.

I turn from the reflection, away from the girl
in the glass. My hand
grips the plastic wand.
I am as ready as I will
ever be.

Acknowledgements

Before I get to the people who helped so wonderfully during the process of writing this book, I feel I really must chastise the individual who initially held it up with a combination of pessimism, doubt and fretting. (Yes. That would be me.)

The thing was, this subject, for reasons both general and personal, was not an easy one to write about. I did not want to be unequal to the task, which at times felt large and weighty. Eventually, I realized all I could do — all any writer can ever do, is offer a voice, craft the words, and trust them to speak where and when and how they are needed. And so that is what I've done.

In part at least, that happened because my publisher and editor, Barry Jowett, saw possibility in a small, early sample I sent to him. He offered the kind of encouragement I needed at that time. And, through the various stages his guidance and confidence in the story kept me on track. Thank you, Barry.

Sarah Jensen did an excellent job on the copy-edit — thanks, Sarah. And indeed the whole team at DCB/Cormorant did all the behind-the-scenes things (some of which remain a mystery to me to this day) efficiently and well. Thank you all!

And thank you, thank you, family and friends, for your love and steadfast presence in my life. I am so richly blessed.

VALERIE SHERRARD was born in 1957 in Moose Jaw, Saskatchewan, and grew up in various parts of Canada. Her father was in the Air Force so the family moved often, and was sent to live in Lahr, West Germany, in 1968. There, her sixth-grade teacher, Alf Lower, encouraged her toward writing, although many years would pass before she began to pursue it seriously.

Valerie's debut YA novel was published in 2002. Since then, she has expanded her writing to include stories for children of all ages.

Valerie Sherrard's work has been recognized on national and international levels and has been translated into several languages. She has won or been shortlisted for numerous awards, including the Governor General's Award for Children's Literature, the Canadian Library Association Book of the Year for Children, the TD Canadian Children's Literature Award, the Geoffrey Bilson, the Ann Connor Brimer, and a wide range of readers' choice awards.

Valerie currently makes her home in New Brunswick with her husband, Brent, who is also an author.

We acknowledge the sacred land on which Cormorant Books operates. It has been a site of human activity for 15,000 years. This land is the territory of the Huron-Wendat and Petun First Nations, the Seneca, and most recently, the Mississaugas of the Credit River. The territory was the subject of the Dish With One Spoon Wampum Belt Covenant, an agreement between the Iroquois Confederacy and Confederacy of the Ojibway and allied nations to peaceably share and steward the resources around the Great Lakes. Today, the meeting place of Toronto is still home to many Indigenous people from across Turtle Island. We are grateful to have the opportunity to work in the community, on this territory.

We are also mindful of broken covenants and the need to strive to make right with all our relations.